ISBN 978-0-259-80700-1
PIBN 10826034




FB &c Ltd, Dalton House, 60 Windsor Avenue, London, SW19 2RR.
Company number 08720141. Registered in England and Wales.

# MUSICAL TRAVELS

THROUGH

# ENGLAND.

BY

JOEL COLLIER, ORGANIST.

Nam, adhuc per domum, aut hortos cecinerat; quos ut parùm celebres, et tantæ voci angustos, spernebat. Non tamen ROMÆ incipere ausus.

TAC.

LONDON:

Printed for G. KEARSLY, in Fleet-street.

M. DCC. LXXIV.

( Price One Shilling. )

[S]aid to be written by Mr Bick[nell]

THROUGH

vide Boswell's

E N G L A N D [Life of Johnson]

Beckford Esqr had some

[share] in it, particularly the

[latter] part

BY

JOEL COLLIER, ORGANIST.

[illegible]am, illinc per domum, aut hortos cecinerat; quos ut
parum celebre, et tantæ voci angustos, spernebat,
[illegible] tamen Romæ incipere ausus.

TAC.

LONDON:

Printed for G. KEARSLY, in Fleet-street.

M.DCC.LXXIV.

( Price One Shilling. )

TO THE

# GOVERNORS of the HOSPITAL for the Maintenance and Education of exposed and deserted young Children.

GENTLEMEN,

*WHILE I was extracting the following sheets from my voluminous Journal, and connecting them together as accurately as I was able, in order to present the Public with a Specimen of my laborious investigation of the present state of* MUSIC *in this my native country, I was somewhat at a loss to whom I could with most propriety inscribe my work. Whether to* DOCTOR BURNEY, *as the original inventor of this species of composition, and the first musical traveller of our nation, to whom I stand so much indebted for the plan, and conduct of my book, and of whom I might truly say in his own words, " that*

 *he*

*he has long been my* magnus Apollo :"—*or whether I was in duty bound to pay homage to the King of* Pruffia, *as the greatest* Dilettante *performer of the age; who, I suppose, at this present writing, like another* Nero, *is playing his new* Solfeggi *to the dying groans of the obstinate* Dantziggers; —*or whether I ought not to call forth from his obscurity that venerable Judge, who contented with less ambitious pleasures, cultivates the fine arts by humbler and modester, but not less curious experiments, and amuses the leisure hours of a long vacation in* caponizing blackbirds *; *or whether I should not do well to express my gratitude, and that of the nation, to the honourable Directors of our Opera, for having at last condescended to permit an* Englishwoman *to be called* Signora, *and by virtue of that title to share some of the princely incomes which have been hitherto lavished on* Italians, *and which, I dare say, those worthy Noblemen and Gentlemen would as readily bestow upon* Englishmen, *if they would but consent to be properly* qualified. *This dilemma, however,*

* Vide the last Vol. of the *Philosophical Transactions.*

*was*

*was at an end, as ſoon as I learnt, that Dr.* Burney, *and Signor* Giardini, *had, under your authority, juſt founded a ſchool for muſic (in imitation, I ſuppoſe, of the Italian* Conſervatorios) *in the* FOUNDLING HOSPITAL, *where about an hundred of ſuch poor children, as have hitherto been placed out to trades and ſervices, in which they had no opportunity of making* a noiſe *in the world, are, in future, to be trained to harmony from their infancy, and conſtantly employed in the ſtudy of muſic; 'till in proceſs of time they take their regular degrees as* Doctors, *and* Doctoreſſes *of muſic, and come forth, ſufficiently accompliſhed (as they muſt be under ſuch maſters,) to form the national taſte, by the true* Italian *ſtandard. When I was informed of this event, I hailed the happy omen, the dawn of an* Auguſtan æra; *and reſolved to offer my tribute of congratulation and applauſe, and to dedicate this work to a ſet of gentlemen, who have ſo diſtinguiſhed their zeal for the intereſt and advancement of muſic. Perhaps it will at firſt appear a bold undertaking in the guardians of deſerted orphans, chiefly ſupported by parliamentary grants of public money, to declare, that they*

*cannot*

*cannot be maintained by the public for a more useful purpose, than to be taught to sing and play* Italian *airs. For men of narrow and contracted minds, who have neither* ear, *nor* voice, *nor* hand, *will still imagine, that it might prove of more national utility, to breed these adopted children of the public, to Husbandry, Navigation, &c. the objects of their original destination; than to convert one of the noblest of our public charities into a nursery for the supply of musical performers at our Theatres, gardens, and shops.—But this is a vulgar prejudice. The improvement of the fine arts ought to be the first object of public attention in an age of luxury,* PEACE, *and plenty, like the present; when we have rivalled the* Italians *in music, it will be time enough to think of our navy, and our agriculture. We have already (to our shame be it spoken.) better sailors than fidlers, and more farmers than* contrapuntists. *But as I take this circumstance to arise entirely from the different degree of encouragement those occupations have hitherto received; I do not despair of seeing the reverse take place, when gentlemen of your rank deign to stand forward, and correct the errors of*

*the*

*the public, by the influence and sanction of your example. Should any obstacles arise to impede the immediate execution of your plan, from some obsolete but unrepealed parliamentary restrictions, doubtless the same legislators who so readily expended the public money in the purchase of Sir* William Hamilton's collection *of antique vases, and* Etruscan *rarities, will not only repeal any former act which may stand in your way; but rejoice in a fresh opportunity of displaying their fine taste and love of the arts; by laying an additional tax upon such of the necessaries of life as are not already overloaded, in order to raise a competent sum for the purchase of the best* Cremonas, *and other instruments which can be procured on the continent, for the service of your* Academia. *I have only to add, gentlemen, that if upon a perusal of the following sheets you shall find, as I am persuaded you will, that my travels are also * in some measure, a matter of national concern; I hope you will be kind enough to second my intended application to parlia-*

* —"He was the first who seemed to think my journey "was, in some measure, a matter of national concern."

Tour to Germany, &c.

*ment,*

*ment; that the charges of my future expeditions may be defrayed at the public expence. This, gentlemen, may be done by a very ſhort clauſe; and as it will enable me to purſue my enquiries with ſpirit, credit, and ſucceſs, will lay a laſting obligation upon,*

*Gentlemen,*

*Your very obedient,*

*and devoted humble Servant,*

JOEL COLLIER.

# MUSICAL TRAVELS, &c.

I WAS born in the Pariſh of *Gotham*, in the county of *Nottingham*: my father was a ſawyer, and my mother had, for many years before her marriage, cried oyſters and Newcaſtle-ſalmon about the ſtreets of London. Neither of them are ſaid to have been remarkable for their vocal or inſtrumental talents. My mother's voice was, indeed, exceedingly ſhrill and diſſonant, as I have been credibly informed by the neighbours; however, I was no ſooner born than I gave proofs of uncommon muſical propenſities. I entered the world, ſinging, inſtead of crying; at leaſt, my ſquall was truly melodious, and raviſhed the ears of the midwife; tho', I muſt confeſs, the envious old hag of a nurſe did pretend that my mother and Mrs. *Midnight* miſtook the origin of the wild notes I uttered as ſoon as I ſaw the light; and, inſiſting that they only denoted the wind-cholic, immediately drenched me with a large doſe of rhubarb: however, ſhe has candidly confeſſed, that ſhe eaſily ſang me to ſleep whenever I was peeviſh; and that even by means of ſuch ſimple melody as *Jack Sprat*, or *hey diddle diddle, the cat and the fiddle*. A harſh and menacing recitative would as effectually deter me from a naughty trick, as a good whipping. The ſound of a drum, or any other martial muſic, had ſuch an immediate effect upon my nerves, that I was always obliged to be turned dry before the piece was half over. The famous *March in Saul* is too powerful for me even at this day, tho' I can ſtand any other, without being offenſive. Indeed, I am ſo well convinced of the connection between the ſound and the ſenſe in all good muſic, that I will venture to preſcribe *Handel's water-piece*, and *water parted from the ſea*, as ſpecifics for a ſtrangury. I know that there is great truth in what *Shakeſpear* ſays of the bag-pipe; and I have obſerved that a jockey always whiſtles to his horſe upon theſe occaſions, which never fails to produce great effects, tho' the performer want brilliancy of execution ever ſo much.

One of the firſt circumſtances I myſelf can recollect in my early years, was the great pleaſure I took in hearing a blind boy play tunes on a bladder of air preſs'd between a bow-ſtick and its ſtring. The Jew's-harp next engaged my attention; and afterwards the bag-pipe and baſſoon. Indeed I do remember having been told by my Grandmother, that whilſt I was yet in coats, I took vaſt delight in pinching the tails of the Parſon's litter of pigs, and would liſten to their various notes and tones from the *f* ſharp of the whine of the leaſt of the family, quite down to the *b* flat of the boar himſelf. This, with my attention to my coral and bells, and rattle, ſinging thro' a comb and brown paper, together with the great expertneſs I afterwards ſhew'd in making whiſtles of reeds, and the recent bark of ſycamore twigs, made the oldeſt people of the pariſh foretel, that I ſhould one day or other become a great and celebrated Muſician.

My taſte for the ſiſter art of muſic, Poetry, was likewiſe, as I am inform'd, obſerved very early in my childhood; as I always held my mouth wide open, when the Pſalm was ſang at our Pariſh-Church; and ſoon was able to repeat without book a great part of *Sternhold* and *Hopkins*'s excellent verſion of that great Dilettanti performer on the harp, King *David*'s pieces.

Having been well inform'd that the infancy, and indeed the riper years of the

great

great Muſ. D. or muſical Doctor (whom I call, *par excellence*, Dr. Mus) paſſed in much the ſame manner, and with ſimilar expectations from all the old ladies of his acquaintance; and having obſerved with what *eclat*, and indeed univerſal approbation of all people of taſte, his ingenious account of his ingenious travels has been received, I conceived a deſign of following ſo illuſtrious an example, and travelling through the dominions of *England, Scotland* and *Ireland*, with the town of *Berwick* upon *Tweed*, to give a true ſtate of the muſical improvement and progreſſion in theſe kingdoms; and hope I may flatter myſelf, that the Dr. himſelf will applaud my undertaking, and conſider it as a proper ſupplement to his elaborate work.

Before I ſet forwards on my travels, I choſe to change my name from *Collier* to *Coglioni* or *Collioni*, as more euphonious; and on the firſt of April, having torn myſelf from the arms of my weeping wife, and four ſmall children, I put my

baſſoon

baſſoon into a green-bag, and flung it acroſs my ſhoulders; my large violoncello was laid on my knee as I ſat in the waggon, and my clothes, with a bottle of brandy and ſome biſcuits, were pack'd up in the viol-caſe. As I was neither patronized, nor franked on my tour by any Dilettanti Lord, I muſt confeſs the low ſtate of my circumſtances, and the poverty in which I had left my family, caſt a damp on my ſpirits; but this was always ſoon diſſipated by an air on the violoncello, and by recollecting the great advantages my travels, to enquire into the ſtate of muſic in this iſland, would be to my dear native country, and the fame and glory I ſhould acquire by the publication of my work, perhaps only inferior to that of the great Dr. *Mus* himſelf.

Inſpir'd by taſte, o'er lands and ſeas HE flew,
Europe he ſaw, and Europe ſaw him too.
Thro' lands of ſinging, or of dancing ſlaves,
Love-ecchoing woods, and lute-reſounding waves.
O, while along the ſtream of time, that name,
Expanded flies, and gathers all its fame;
Say, ſhall my little bark attendant ſail,
Purſue the triumph and partake the gale?

LIN-

# LINCOLN.

THUS occaſionally conſoling myſelf, the waggon arrived at the famous and ancient city of *Lincoln*. My firſt viſit was to a young lady of high muſical acquirements. She received me with a moſt bewitching air, which ſhe ſang to her guittar, for ſhe had heard of my fame at *Gotham*, and was not unapprized of my ambulatory deſign: her name was originally *Fernihough*, but ſhe had long dropped the *hough* at the end of it, as gothic and inharmonious. Thus ſhe ſaluted me:

"Dear Collioni, Collioni, Collioni;
Dear, dear, dear, Collioni;
Happy, happy, Gotham, Gotham;
Gotham, Gotham, happy Gotham."

I could only bow and ſmile in anſwer to this compliment, (which indeed, tho' very elegant, I did not conceive was above my merits,) as I had not an extempore ſonnet ready made to anſwer it.

Then

Then taking my hand with a delightful air, ſhe introduced me to Dr. *Dilettanti*, a moſt illuſtrious timeiſt; he ſat muſing and beating with his foot, and took hold of, and quitted my hand in the ſame portion of time, which he meaſured by the pulſations of his foot.

" Excuſe, ſaid he, illuſtrious *Collioni*, " the meaſured mode of my geſtures in " ſaluting you; but I have long ac- " cuſtomed myſelf to meaſure out the parts " of time on a variety of ſounding inſtru- " ments, and have at length introduced it " into all the motions of my body. At " my houſe, ſir, you will learn to cut your " meat, and move your jaws at dinner in " common or triple time, according to " the inſtruments that accompany our " meals.——By dealing the cards at qua- " drille, how eaſy it is to judge if the " party has an ear!——yonder gentleman " who comes towards our window, ſee how " he ſwings his arms in exact time, true as " the pendulum of a clock. I can aſſure

" you

" you, sir, he is great on the violoncello.
" My dear wife says, the conjugal endear-
" ments are doubly improved, if a husband
" is a good timeist. She approves of
" triple time; and on this account I for-
" merly had a servant who play'd in our
" bed-room every Sunday night, 'till we
" slept. And since I became one of the
" *castrati*, I have acquired the habit of
" making water at intervals in the truest
" time like a pig; and may say, that I
" believe for exactness of ear, that I am
" not exceeded by any modern musician."

On this, this great man took up a Jew's harp that lay by him, and with a twing, twang, twong, moving his finger across his lips, and making faces in the most exact time, he fetched out such prurient harmony, as ravished my very soul, and threw sweet Miss *Ferni* into the most agreeable convulsions.

During our dinner, two of the Doctor's servants entertained us with many excellent and solemn pieces of music. Indeed,

I was so solicitous to cut and eat my meat in true time, as I thought my character depended on this circumstance, that I unfortunately cut my lips, so that the blood much terrified me; and sweet Miss *Ferni* was so earnestly attending to the fiddlers, that on their suddenly changing the time from *adagio* to *festina*, she swallowed the ivory spoon out of a mustard pot; which, as it stuck across her throat, I am sure must have given that excellent young lady exquisite pain, yet did she cough, and even vomit repeatedly in most accurate time, and screamed from fear most harmoniously through the whole gamut, from *a* to *g* inclusively, long after the spoon was restored to its place.

SHEF-

# SHEFFIELD.

DR. *Dilettanti* was so kind as to make me a present of a place in the stage coach to *Sheffield* in my road to *York*, that I might inquire into the present state of the music of that city and cathedral. Amongst the other passengers, was a gentleman of a grave aspect; who, from his not attending to me at the inn, when I play'd a most inchanting solo on my hautboy, appear'd at first to have no ears, but on further conversation I found him a most agreeable companion. He cry'd up the ingenuity of the *Sheffield* manufacturers, and told me of a new musical instrument, more complicate, he thought, and louder than an organ. The next day he was so good as to accompany me to hear this new organic instrument. The first thing I could observe was a number of iron pipes, and a water wheel to work the large bellows, like that organ of which there is a print in *Kempleri Musurgia*. When the wheel was in motion, I obſerved many of the notes higher than in any organ I had ever heard; and was told, that theſe ingenious people had found the only way to produce theſe was, by boring gun-barrels: to theſe a ſymphony was adduced by files which cut the teeth of large ſaws, and the mellow tones of two great hammers, which at intervals ſtruck on large pieces of red-hot iron, made a more tremendous and affecting concert, than all the mingled whiſtles of *Cecilia's* organ.

Having paid a ſhilling to the performers of this ſtupendous piece of harmony, at which my grave companion ſeem'd much delighted, and liſten'd to my remarks upon it with the greateſt avidity and approbation; " Signior *Callioni*," ſays he, " your obſervations inchant me; the moſt " antient muſic, as you well explain, was " made with hammers beating upon an-

" vils,

"vils, as invented by *Tubal Cain*, and "practiſed in the ſhop of his ſucceſſor, "*Vulcan*, 'tho' *Saturn* is thought to have "been the firſt of the *caſtrati*.—But this "invention was not compleat, Signior "*Collioni*, it was not compleat, till this "excellent treble made by boring guns, "and cutting ſaws was added.—It is now "become the true antient, celebrated, "long-loſt, and long-deplored chromatic, "which that *Heathen*, *Plato*, who had "doubtleſs aſs's ears, expelled from his "artificial commonwealth."

"Doubtleſs you are right in your con-"jectures, reply'd I, Mr. *Hummings*, "(for that was my kind companion's "name) it was muſic like this, which "could diſenchant the moon, and make "trees and ſtones dance *allemands*. "Would you believe it, Mr. *Hummings*, "I once cured a girl bit with a tarantula "myſelf with this ſimple baſſoon?

"*Trut, turrut, phub, phub, buſh!*— "This was the air, Mr. *Hummings*, you "ſhall

" ſhall hear it——*trut, turrut, phub, phub,* " *buſh*:—the girl riſing from her melan- " lancholy attitude, danced till the ſweat " ran down to the hem of her ſcarlet " petticoat; and after I had preſented her " with a bit of money, became ſo lively " as to ſtrip herſelf like King *David*, and " danced like a *Heinel*. I can aſſure you, " Mr. *Hummings*, I drove away the evil " ſpirit, and cured her of her tarantuliſm " that night.

"Not unlike this, is a fact recorded " by the divine *Homer*. *Ulyſſes* had a " large rent made in his thigh by a wild " boar,—a terrible animal, Mr. *Hum-* " *mings*:—well, and what happen'd?— " why, he only ſent for the town-waits, " and after the firſt bar or two were " play'd, the blood ſtopp'd; and as the " fiddles proceeded, the wound con- " tracted, and by the time they had " finiſhed *Alley Croaker*, *Moggy Lauder*, " and *A lovely Laſs to a Fryar came*, (which " are all antient *Greek* tunes, ſir,) the

" wound

"wound was quite healed, and the "cicatrix as smooth as the back of my "hand."

During this conversation, an unfortunate accident had happened near us. One of the performers on the hammer and iron by a fall had broken his leg. A surgeon was sent for with all dispatch, but Mr. *Hummings* said I had as well try the effect of the bassoon upon him; and pointing to me, told the people that they need seek no farther, for I was superior to any surgeon. Upon this, untying my green bag, the man cry'd out, he begg'd no instruments might be used. "No, (says "I,) none but a musical instrument." So I began with a gentle blast, and played and sung alternately,—"*You'll ne'er go* "*the sooner to the Stygian Ferry. Let not* "*your noble spirits be cast down, but drink* "*drink, drink, and be merry.*"—"Give "me some ale, (cries the wounded man) "I like this, Doctor." Afterward I blew till I nearly had burst my cheeks, and then ſung, *If 'tis joy to wound a lover*; but the bone would not knit:—indeed I could not make it knit at all—and I don't believe, as Mr. *Hummings* ſaid, that if Dr. *Mus* himſelf, and all the muſicians of Britain, fiddlers, violoncellos, double violoncellos, trumpets, and trumpet-marinos, together with every *Maeſtro di Capella* in *Italy* had been preſent, they could have made this bone knit—which, I ſuppoſe, was owing to the ſcorbutic habit of body of the patient; indeed, Mr. *Hummings* attributed it entirely to this cauſe; for the blood ſtopped before I had finiſhed the firſt ſong.

YORK.

## YORK.

NOTHING worth remark occur'd in my journey from hence to *York*; but at my approach to this celebrated city, my heart leapt for joy as ſoon as I beheld the towers of the cathedral; here, ſays I, I ſhall be much careſſed and followed, I dare believe, as there are ſo many of the *Dilettanti* who reſide within the precincts of this antient ſeat of muſic and ſuperſtition. This letter, ſays I, is of ineſtimable value, taking it from my pocket, and reading the direction, "For that incomparable "Muſician and Antiquarian, Dr. *Hiccup*;" doubtleſs he will pay great attention to his friends at *Lincoln*, who have honoured me with it. The footman ſhewed me into an elegant parlour, where there was a clock with chimes, ſo contrived that St. *Peter*, St. *Paul*, and the *Virgin Mary* were ſeen ſtriking alternately on the bells, and by a ſweet trio announced every hour of the day. Dr. *Hiccup* was, it ſeems, at his devotions, which he always performed in imitation of that great and devout muſician, King *David*. He was a tall, boney figure, with a ſwarthy complexion, and blear eyes. As I ſat down he took no notice of me, but continued dancing with a harp in his hand, without his breeches, and with his night-gown and ſhirt tucked up above his waiſt; and as he turned his brown poſteriors this way and that, in the gyrations of the dance, all the women and children that were looking in through the window of his parlour, giggled, and made faces; and ſhewed variety of indecent geſticulations and noiſes. None of theſe, however, interrupted the devotions of this great man.

Never were ſuch charming tunes elicited from mortal harp, *Cambrian* or *Eolic!* the dance was Devotion itſelf in human form! After a little refreſhment, this illuſtrious Muſician condeſcended to enter-

tain

tain me with ſeveral intereſting particulars of the manner of his life, which I begg'd leave to copy in my pocket book in his preſence.

He roſe every morning, when his chime-clock ſtruck eleven, (for, like the famous *Chevalier Gluck*, he is too great a genius to riſe early) and generally gaped all the time his lady was putting on his breeches. For breakfaſt he always eat rolls and butter, whether in ſummer or winter; and after his breakfaſt paid a viſit to *Cloacina*, but aſſured me he never uſed old muſic books on this occaſion on any account. He retired to reſt about ten, and ſeldom fail'd once in a month to compliment his lady for undreſſing him.

He communicated many other particulars to me of leſs moment, and was ſo obliging at length to beg I would treat him with an air or two on the baſſoon.

I thought this a good opportunity to give him a ſpecimen of my poetic talents, as well as of my muſical ones, and performed the following ſong, which I compoſed at *Gotham* ſeveral years ago.

> "Some came in a waggon, and ſome in a cart;
> And many there were that did nothing but f—t:
> Oh rare *Nottingham* town, *Nottingham* town!
> *Nottingham* town; Oh rare *Nottingham* town!"

The ſweetneſs of the notes on my baſſoon, an inſtrument whoſe tone is ſo like the ſound it was to repreſent, raviſhed his ears, which he hung quite down on each ſhoulder, during the whole time of my performance.

I ſlept this night at Dr. *Hiccup*'s houſe, and borrowed a ſhirt and pair of ſtockings of him. At breakfaſt I took an opportunity to tell him of the narrowneſs of my circumſtances; but he was ſuddenly taken with a rapturous fit of devotion, and pulling up his night-gown to his waiſt, began to ſing, and dance, and caper, and kick, to ſuch a degree, that no one in the room was ſafe: I ran towards the door to ſave my ſhins, and the Doctor riſing with both feet in the air like a Harlequin, gave me ſuch a horſe-kick on my rump, ſinging

ſinging at the ſame time the *March in Saul*, that I deſcended into the ſtreet down five ſteps, head foremoſt, and cracked my baſſoon in twenty places.

Six hours I attended at the door, but was told by a ſervant out of a window, that the Doctor was ſtill performing his dance of devotion; and for aught I know, that great man may dance till doom's-day, as I never after could get any other anſwer at his door.

On more mature reflexion, I thought this kind of treatment very hard from a brother muſician, and one to whom I was ſo well recommended; but I conſoled myſelf with conſidering, that though my baſſoon was broken in ſundry places, yet I had retained the Doctor's ſhirt and ſtockings; and that it was very likely my great prototype, Dr. Mus himſelf, had frequently met with the ſame treatment, tho' his modeſty had inclined him to conceal it.

## DURHAM.

FROM this place to *Durham* I was necessitated to travel on foot; and by playing the *Black Joke*, *Murdoch O'Blaney*, and other sentimental tunes to the girls of the villages I pass'd through, procured food and lodging, which my brother of the String had refused me. At *Darlington*, I waited on the *Maestro di Capella*, or clerk of the parish, who I may assert had the finest nasality, or nose-intonation, that ever was given to *David*'s *psalms*; and the melody of his *Amen*, was quite astonishing.

So well was my bassoon received at this church, that the 'Squire's lady invited me to Dinner. "Good Signior *Collioni*," says "she, you have charmed, you have en-"raptured me; pray, has the wind which "escapes out at the end of your instrument "any smell?"——"smell! says I, no, "madam,

"madam, not unless I eat onions." At this all the ladies laughed most extravagantly.

However, the 'Squire after dinner gave me a recommendatory letter to the great Mr. *Eccho* of *Durham*, principal performer belonging to that opulent cathedral; and withal told me, that Mr. *Eccho* had so long apply'd himself to musical notes, that he had utterly forgot all articulate language. That he preached, conversed, prayed, scolded, swore, talk'd bawdy, and blasphemy, all on the fiddle, without uttering a word, or even making a sign with his fingers.

At my introduction to this great man, I began a long complimental speech, which I had been some time studying.—— "Most respectable sir, whose soul is a "soul of harmony, and whose body is "like a base-viol."——Here he snatch'd up his fiddle with an air of great complacency, and drawing the bow gently over the strings said, as plain as if he had

ſpoke it. "Oh, ſir, your moſt obedient;
" you compliment me indeed, ſir, too
" much." I then told him how long a journey I had performed on foot, and that the duſty roads had made me dry. He ſnatched up his violin, and before he had play'd above a bar or two, in came a footman with a jug of delicate ale. Next I mentioned modeſtly my having eat nothing all day.——"*Trut, trut, biſh, baſh, buſh,*" cries the fiddle—" Indeed, ſir, replies I, I,
" don't faſt for the ſake of devotion"——
"*ir, er, ar, querr, quorr, quurr*"—quoth the fiddle, and in came a ſurloin of cold beef, and muſtard and bread, in the twinkling of a fiddle-ſtick.

This gentleman, quoth I, is greater than *Orpheus* or *Eurydice*, or the *Serpent*;—no, no, *Orpheus* could do no ſuch things as theſe—ale and beef were a note or two above his fiddle!

Soon after came in Mr. *Eccho*'s wife, with a " what the deuce are you about;
" bringing beggars into my houſe?"—Mr.

*Eccho*

*Eccho* catched up the fiddle, and ſuch a jar did I never hear "*arg, erg, urg, gir,* "*gor, gur*"—I warrant you madam became as dumb as if ſhe were inchanted.

Indeed, hearing this lady give me the opprobrious name of beggar, I took care to ſhew the diamond ring on my little finger, which I always wear when I perform in public, which might give her a better opinion of me, tho' indeed it is only a Briſtol ſtone, and that I pay a ſilver-ſmith two pence a week for the uſe of; and I would have hired a laced waiſtcoat, but was aſked a ſhilling a week, tho' I am ſure the lace had been twice turn'd; yet, if I had hired it, I dare ſay Dr. *Hiccup* would ſcarcely have kicked me out of his houſe.

## CARLISLE.

AT *Carlisle* I waited on Lord *Diddle-doodle* with proper musical credentials: he was sat against a glass practising some solfeggis on the violin, and attending to the gracefulness of his own attitude. "Most illustrious Peer, "says I," (making a bow to the very ground) "your noble ancestors gain'd "victory in the hardy fields of war, but "you by music civilize and harmonize "mankind; with what rapture must they "lean from their starry mansions to see "and hear your immortal powers of har- "mony and grace!" I stopp'd, and on looking up, found that his lordship had not attended to a word I had spoken, nor seemed conscious of my being in the room;—but as great geniuses are often absent, I repeated my compliment in a louder voice, and approaching, was

amazed

amazed to find that his lordſhip was quite deaf, deaf as a poſt; and yet he executed the moſt difficult paſſages in muſic with the greateſt grace and manner, better, I dare ſay, than if he had heard his own performance.

When his lordſhip had perceived me, he approached me with the utmoſt politeneſs, and made ſigns for me to ſit down, and accompany him upon the baſſoon, which I did 'till dinner-time. After dinner, I intreated my lady *Diddle-doodle* to prevail upcn the noble lord to ſing, which he did; but I was rather diſappointed at finding that his voice was only packthread *. However, he ſung in tune; had a ſhake, and was far from vulgar. My lady afterwards made ample amends by her own ſinging.. Her voice was a ſkane of ſilk, without the leaſt mixture of worſted. She underſtood all the lights and ſhades of melody. Her back-ground;

* "His voice is now but a thread."
TOUR TO ITALY.

her mezzotints; and her clare-obſcure were charming, and there was ſuch a roundneſs and dignity in all the tones, that every thing ſhe did became intereſting.

It was in this part of *England*, I paid a viſit to Mr. *Quaver*, with recommendatory letters from lord *Diddle-doodle*; I found him to be a gentleman of conſiderable and original muſical genius; his taſte was pure, chaſte, refined; and his execution, particularly upon the Jew's harp, was exquiſite; he executed with great taſte and powers, *Nancy Dawſon*, *Lilla-bullero*, and *Old Sir Simon the king*. After dinner he explained to me his ſyſtem for the improvement of ſound, which was at once ſublime and original. " The Author " of Nature," ſaid he, " has with an equal " and judicious hand diſtributed his gifts " among his creatures: to one he has given " ſtrength; to another, dexterity; to a third, " perſeverance; in the ſame manner has he " divided the agreeable qualifications; and

" the

" the courtier and the fine gentleman need " not blush to receive instruction from the " spaniel and the monkey—Now as the " philosopher models his life upon an imi- " tation of the virtues of animals, the true " connoisseur will do the same"—there he stopp'd, as if afraid to explain himself; but I told him, that there was something so original and masterly in his conceptions that I should never be easy, until he communicated them. Upon which, after a short pause, he seized me by the hand, and grasping it with affection, " since, " said he, I find in you the true spirit of " your science, I will no longer maintain " any reserve; know then, that after a " profound meditation upon the sublimest " mysteries of our profession, I have traced " them up to the creation"—" how! said " I, with amaze, I thought that the greatest " Antiquarians had never brought them " with any certainty higher than the De- " luge." " I knew," said he, " I should sur- " prize you; but it is certain that *Adam*,

" amongst

" amongst his other qualifications, possessed " that of expressing every sound that ever " has or can be uttered; hence he could not " only sing base and treble, counter-tenor, " and soprano to admiration; but also " squeak like a pig, croak like a frog, bel- " low like a bull, whinny like a colt, and " bray like an ass.

" It is true, that the greater part of these " faculties was taken from him at the Fall, " and have been very sparingly bestowed " upon his descendants; from hence arises " that degeneracy into which music has " fallen in the modern ages of the world: " that sublime science, instead of expressing " the natural passions, by a judicious imita- " tion of the tones of beasts; instead of " roaring out the lion's rage; bellowing the " jealousy of the bull, or chanting the amo- " rous passions of the nightingale, is become " a meer unmeaning jargon, without force, " or energy, and its professors and ad- " mirers are dwindled into the most con- " temptible part of the creation; quavering

" eunuchs, unfeeling prostitutes, insignifi-
" cant blockheads, wretches without head,
" or heart, or sentiment, or enthusiasm."—
I was too sensible that there was but too much truth in this gentleman's observations, though I could not assent to every thing he said against our modern *virtuosi*, among whom envy itself must acknowledge there are some accomplished characters; and the eighteenth century will always glory in having produced an ELECTOR of MUNICH, a TENDUCCI, and a MUS.

" But," said my friend, " perceiving
" this to be the lamentable state of things,
" I have with true and indefatigable in-
" dustry applied myself to the restoration
" of the first *Adamitical* harmony; I have
" selected the most admirable notes from
" every animal, and have already acquired
" a tolerable proficiency in bellowing,
" braying and grunting: I indeed found
" that the *squall* of the peacock was two
" notes too high for my voice; but in re-

" turn,

"turn, if I may ſay ſo without vanity, I "can inſpire every hen and goſling in the "yard with tender ſentiments. I have, "beſides this, collected every great natu- "ral genius that I have found among the "brute creation; I have a young he-aſs "who has an admirable baſs; a young "hog, (a *caſtrato*) who ſings counter- "tenor; and a dear little cat, whom, in "honour of that illuſtrious name, ſo ce- "lebrated in the Doctor's tour, I call "MINGOTTI, who has an excellent tre- "ble, and a ſurpriſing *portamento*. But "why waſte I time in deſcription? you "ſhall ſee my ſcholars, and my *ſchola*."

Saying this, he led me to a large building, which reſembled a barn, where we were received by the *Maeſtro di Capella*, who was an old and deaf huntſman. The firſt object I beheld was a beautiful ſhe-aſs in a *Mecklinburgh* night-cap, who brayed a ſolo. Her voice was one of the cleareſt, ſweeteſt, trueſt, moſt powerful and extenſive I ever heard. In compaſs, it it is from *Bb* on the fifth ſpace in the baſs, to *D* in *alt*, full ſteady and equal; her ſhake was good, and her *portamento* admirably free from the noſe, mouth, or throat. We were then entertained by a duet between the *Mingotti*, and a large raven, in the *chromatic*, which grew more ſpirited by my friend's pulling a bone out of his pocket, which he threw to the performers, and thereby produced a *conflicta*. I then told my friend that I would willingly hear the *caſtrato*, but he told me he was afraid the *Caffarelli* could not oblige me in that particular, as he had unfortunately taken cold by rolling too long upon an unaired dunghill, and was then actually in a courſe of ſugar-candy. However, he threw a turnip to encourage him to exert himſelf, and I could judge from what I then heard, that he is likely to become a moſt maſterly performer.

My friend then tied ſtrings to the ears of ſix young greyhound puppies, which he twitch'd with ſo much art and judgment by means of a pully, that I think the effect was equal to any *viol di gamba* I ever heard, not excepting that of the Elector of *Munich*.

My friend then suspended two cats by the tails, which he contrived should alternately bob upon the noses of two sucking pigs, who were tied by the hind-legs to the floor: though I observed these performers were somewhat embarassed in their manner, yet I could not but acknowledge the effect was quite original and truly theatric.

Mr. *Quaver* then told me that he had formerly introduced some of these performers to sing at a concert, but without success: and he made great complaints of the unpoliteness of the audience, which he said could sit with patience three hours to listen to the unmeaning trills of heroes in hoop-petticoats, and *Italian* vagabonds in a strange language, while they would not bestow one half hour upon the voice of nature and their brethren. Tho'. I was quite ignorant of the facts he alluded too, yet, like Dr. Mus, I was so partial to talents, wherever I found them, that I could not help condoling with my kind host upon the occasion; and after having bemoaned the degeneracy of the times, and wished him success in his truly original undertaking, which I promised him I would take due notice of in my intended work, I set forward on my journey to *Bristol*.

Had I been rich, I should have agreed with a coachman, who was just then setting out, and offered to carry me and my bassoon, in the basket, for sixteen shillings. But as riches are not always the companions of genius, I rather chose to take my place in a coal-vessel; which was to arrive at that city in three days. Here, as the weather was extremely fine when I sat out, I travelled very agreeably, for the first day, and dined upon bread and cheese, and cold bacon, without making any observations worth communicating to the public, except that I ſaw a man ſtanding upon the bank, and angling for dace, notwithſtanding the earlineſs of the ſeaſon.

The ſecond day, as the wind ſuddenly changed from Weſt to North-Eaſt, was foggy, rainy, and ſo exceedingly cold, that I was obliged, for want of Dr. Mus's louſy blanket, to ſlip my legs and thighs into a coal-ſack; we ſtopped about two o'clock at *Averley*, a little village on the banks of the *Severn* to dine; and here I cannot but inform the world, that Mr. *Bangor*, at the ſign of the *Goat in Boots*, is an extremely civil and polite landlord, and has no contemptible taſte in muſic. When I informed him of my deſign in making this expedition, he very obligingly led me into his hall, which was ſtuck round with various antique pieces of muſic, ſuch as *Chevy Chace*, *The Children in the Wood*, *Three Children ſliding on the Ice*, *The hiſtory of St. George*, &c. which he kindly permitted me to enrich my collection with. I begged hard

hard that he would permit me to prick out the notes of an incomparable whiſtle as he performed it, which at length with great difficulty he complied with, upon condition however that I ſhould not print it. But I was more than all ſurprized and charmed with his generoſity, in ſlipping a piece of fried cow's heel into my pocket, and inſiſting upon treating me with a dram, before I went into the cold.

As I walked down to the river ſide, I remarked a boy, who was humming the tune of *Yanky Doodle*; and as I knew this to be an extremely popular air in ſome parts of *America*, I conjectured that this part of *England* was originally peopled from that continent.

BRISTOL.

# BRISTOL.

LATE the next evening, we arrived at *Briſtol,* a large and populous city, more famous for its commerce, manufactures and ſuch trifles, than for its taſte in muſic. They have but lately had a regular theatre eſtabliſhed there to civilize and poliſh the uncouth manners of the diſſenters, who would even have ſucceeded in the ſavage oppoſition they made to this ſalutary meaſure, if the biſhops had not eſpouſed the cauſe of the fine arts; I have little doubt, therefore, that they will ſoon find that "muſic is ſo "combined with things ſacred and im-"portant, as well as with our pleaſures, "that it ſeems neceſſary to our ex-"iſtence:" they will then quickly become friends to organs, and next to operas. As I approached the city, I was gratified with ſeeing the battalions of the principal militia,

militia, who made a moſt formidable appearance, and marched in exact time to the marrow-bones and cleavers, which had an admirable effect and were extremely animating. I put up at the *Dog's Head in the Porridge-Pot*, and after powdering my wig with ſome flour, clipping my beard with a pair of ſciſſars, and turning my ſhirt, I went to wait on Signor *Manſelli*, to whom I had letters of recommendation. When I had knocked at the door, and enquired whether the Signor was within, I was informed that he was, but that I could not ſee him, as he was then buſied in performing his vocalities. This anſwer, you may be ſure, redoubled my curioſity, and I replied, "if a poor, yet I truſt, "not unknown muſician, may be judged "worthy of being an unobſerved ſpectator "of the Signor's meditations, I promiſe "not to interrupt his reveries, and per-"haps the Signor himſelf will not be "diſpleaſed at your introducing to him a "*Collioni!*"

When he learned that I was a musician, he bowed respectfully, and desiring me to pull off my shoes, as he did himself, he led me to the Signor's apartment. When we came to the door, the servant desired me to pull off my coat, waistcoat, and wig, and creep through a hole, which he shewed me at the bottom of the door, as he assured me the Signor did not suffer even crowned heads to approach him in these moments of enthusiasm, without taking those precautions; "and sir," said he, "you need not think this an humiliating "situation, as I have seen many persons of "the first fashion, among whom were "several pregnant ladies, submit to the "same ceremony."

I did not hesitate a moment to comply with the customary *etiquette*, but stripping myself to the shirt, I crept into the room with the same awful silence with which the antient priests approached the Tripod of their God: Having posted myself behind a large screen, I beheld the

Signor

Signor extended on his belly, while two young and beautiful ladies were gently ſtroaking his back with the palms of their hands. He lay for ſome minutes penſive and ſilent, as if waiting for the inſpirations of the divinity. At length, on a ſudden, "his eyes were fixt, "his underlip fell, and drops of ef-"ferveſcence diſtilled from his whole "countenance" Immediately exploſions of the moſt muſical intonation I had ever heard, iſſued from behind, and enraptured the whole company. After this, he ſucceſſively coughed, ſneezed, hiccuped, eructated, ſqueaked and whiſtled in the moſt harmonious manner that can be conceived. "Thank heaven," cried the Signor, "my powers of harmony are "yet undiminiſhed: I ſhall ſtill live to "bleſs the world, and poliſh this brutal "nation." Saying this, he took up his fiddle, and played a moſt divine ſolo. I heard him for ſome time in ſilent ecſtacy, 'till at length incapable of ſuppreſſing my emotions any longer, I precipitated myſelf into his arms, crying or rather blubbering out in imitation of the great *Caffarelli*, *Bravo! bravissimo! Manselli, è Collioni che ti lo dice.* The Signor seemed somewhat surprized at my abrupt introduction, but at length, recollecting himself, he received me with ineffable politeness. The ladies at my appearance, had shrieked, and left the room, which in the first hurry of our embraces we had not perceived. But presently the Signor, glancing his eye downwards, recollected himself, and said with some warmth and emphasis, "O, fye, Signor *Collioni*, I "took it for granted you were one of "us." I blushed at the imputation, and said, "I hoped this defect would not "lessen me in his esteem, as my country "was not yet sufficiently civilized to have "adopted the custom; and though some "of our prime nobility had the spirit and "taste to lead the way, yet in the gross "conceptions of the *English*, there was a "certain degree of ridicule annexed to it,

"which

"which deterred several men otherwise "of the most exquisite politeness from "submitting to it." The Signor was kind enough to admit my excuses, but lamented this as the greatest obstacle to the national advancement in the science of music. However, he averred that several *English* young noblemen of fortune had to his knowledge undergone the operation in *Italy*, "and though," added he, "an "ordinary proficient may be exempted "from the practice, yet it is indispensibly "necessary for one who would fathom all "the mysteries of the art, and emulate the "illustrious names of *Senesino*, *Farinelli*, "*Tenducci*, &c."

I confess I was much staggered at what he said, more especially as I began to entertain some doubts myself whether the characters of a man and a musician were at all compatible.

I hinted to him, that I had formerly heard, that a certain great Personage, *tàm Marti quàm Mercurio*, equally illustrious for his martial and his musical talents, had adopted the practice; but as the Doctor had not recorded it in his tour to *Potzdam*, I imagined the report was without foundation.

"Ah!" said he, "depend upon it, tho' "the Doctor has indeed omitted this "circumstance in the admirable descrip- "tion he gives of that hero, and Dilet- "tante practising his *solfeggi* at *Potzdam*, "yet he would never have been either the "monarch, or the flutist he is without it. "Do you think, added he, that illustrious "philosopher could amuse himself so calm- "ly in his closet with fugus and adagios, "while ten thousand *Polish* widows, and "orphans, were imprecating curses upon "the head of their unfeeling destroyer, "unless he had totally disengaged himself "from every incumbrance of his sex "and species?"

Here the entrance of the young ladies interrupted any further conversation on the subject. The eldest, his niece, who was called

*Glucki-*

*Gluckinella Inglesina*, desired me to sing; which I did in the softest and most unmanly tone I could exert, that I might not again offend. I asked her what her real opinion of my voice was? she answered me with the most perfect affability, that I acquitted myself tolerably well *considering*; tho' "she thought me too ambitious of dis-"playing my talent of working parts and "subjects, and added that my *cantilena* "was often rude."

I took an opportunity when I was alone with this young lady, to enquire if the *castrati* were much in vogue at *Bristol*, and if that operation could be so safely attempted on elderly gentlemen; this young lady smiled at my simplicity, and assured me that the operation was safe and easy, and not so painful as to acquire any degree of resolution, and that the *castrati* were the favourites of the ladies, both of the married and unmarried. She advised me by all means to undergo the operation as the Doctor had done in *Italy*, tho' his excess of modesty prevented him from

boasting

boasting of it in his excellent treatise. She added, that she could not with safety love me, unless I would submit to this for her sake.

This declaration from a young lady for whom I now perceived I had imbibed the most ardent affection, gave me great uneasiness; that affection however was purely platonic and spiritual, for personal charms she had no more to boast of, that ever I discovered, than *Mingotti* herself. Besides the disadvantage of a contortion in the ogle, vulgarly called a squint of the eye, and a very long, red nose, she had a mouth, which tho' it opened from ear to ear, discovered to the eye nothing but the sad remains of a set of ebony teeth, which more resembled the ruins of an old cathedral, than the polished ivory which adorns the comic mouth of the celebrated Mrs. *Ab-ngt-n*. There was yet another circumstance to disgust the sensualist, and deter him from approaching this Syren with an improper familiarity; and that was the great offensiveness of her breath,

which

which was ſo violent, that any perſon not "determined" like me "to hear, ſee," and ſmell "nothing but muſic," might have thought it hardly atoned for by the ſweetneſs of her voice. Yet none of theſe circumſtances damped the ardor of my ſpiritual attachment, founded, as it was, upon a ſolid baſis, the love of ſong;—it was embodied harmony, the tuneful ſoul which I adored. The reader who is unacquainted with the difference between a groſs ſenſual paſſion, and a ſublime, harmonic ſympathy, may perhaps be ſurprized when I tell him, that while I was thus devoted to the divine *Gluckinella*, I was at the ſame time perſonally captivated by the corporeal attractions of a little black-ey'd Gypſy, the wife of a barber in the town, who often ſhaved me for a tune; yet did not theſe groſſer feelings the leaſt impair or abate my muſical platonic love. I might perhaps be excuſed, were I to conceal the progreſs and iſſue of theſe different amours; but they are ſo intimately blended wth the ſcientific part of my work, and were attended with ſuch important conſequences to myſelf in my profeſſional capacity, that I doubt not the narration will prove of great utility to my brethren. For it was no common temptation that deluded me; tho' Mrs. *Sharp-ſet* was abundantly handſome, I could have reſiſted "the blandiſhments of beauty," if a deſire of making dangerous experiments upon the power and effects of muſic upon female paſſion had not ſeized my brain. For I had taken notice, that the imagination of this young woman was exceedingly lively, and far out-ſtripped her huſband's, who was a plain dull man with little fire or enthuſiaſm in his compoſition. I plainly perceived this in all her geſtures and movements, but when I ſung ſome tender ſentimental air, her involuntary ſighs, bluſhes, and languid attitude, betrayed too plainly the irritability of her nervs, and that fine ſuſceptibility of ſoft emotions with which nature has

endowed

endowed the ſex. No wonder that in a rude, uncultivated ſtate of nature as I then was, I caught the ſubtle fire from her contagious eyes. Ah! how often did I ſing the *ſweet paſſion of Love* without once thinking of my dear *Gluckinella*; how often did ſhe encore my *O how pleaſing 'tis to pleaſe*, without the ſlighteſt recollection of her abſent barber! Madly determined to purſue the fatal experiment, and obſerve the full effects of my art; I next ſung "*Haſte, let us rove, to the Iſland of* "*Love*", at which Mrs. *Sharpſet* was greatly agitated and danced about the room. Then I played a rapturous voluntary "produced in the happy moments of "effervеſcence when my reaſon was leſs "powerful than my feeling;" and at length I proceeded to ſuch exceſs of temerity, as to tune up *Geho Dobbin*, *Murdoch O'Blaney*, and ſeveral other inflammatory compoſitions; and finding my miſtreſs "attentive, and in a diſpoſition "to be pleaſed, I became animated to

 that

"that true pitch of enthusiasm, which "from the ardor of the fire within, "is communicated to others and sets all "around in a blaze, so that the con- "tention between the performer and "the hearer was only who should please "or who should applaud the most, "till at length, not contented with "shewing her approbation by coughing, "hemming, and blowing the nose," she "expressed rapture in a manner peculiar "to herself, and seemed to agonize with "pleasure too great for the aching "sense!" for at length, overpowered by my quirking and quavering, and transported beyond all the bounds of prudence, Mrs. *Sharpset* on a sudden leaped into my arms, hung round my neck, and devoured me with eager kisses, such as I never tasted before or since. What man, what unemasculated god could have withstood such potent snares? Ah! my serene *Gluckinella* had'st thou been there, these tumults had all subsided, the devil had not got intire

ossession

poſſeſſion of my mind, voice and inſtrument, nor had I needed the painful operation of the barber's avenging ſteel to bring my wandering ſpirits back to reaſon:—for ſoon, and in the midſt of our illicit joys, the door of the chamber was forced open, and in ruſhed Mr. *Sharpſet*.——Diſcordant oaths and curſes, and the look and voice of a Fury making an incantation to awake the dead, beſpoke the injured huſband, and ſcared us from the bed. He retired a moment to fetch the inſtrument of his revenge. Mrs. *Sharpſet* eſcaped, but in an inſtant I ſaw him return whetting his keeneſt razor; and concluding, that he meant to cut my throat upon the ſpot, I fell down at his feet and in an agony of fear and penitence, roared out ſuch a MISERERE, as was never heard at the Pope's chapel in *Paſſion-week*. Alas! how did I wiſh for the genius of a *Gluck*, "to paint *my* difficult ſituation occaſioned "by complicated misery, and the tem-"pestuous fury of unbridled passions!" But *Allegri* himself, had he chanted his own MISERERE, could not have moved the shaver's unrelenting soul, or soothed his injured honour up in arms, and demanding its victim! I tried a softer strain, and sang in melting mood, "*Let not rage thy* "*Bosom firing, pity's softer claim remove,*" &c. but it was all one: still strapped he his inexorable razor, humming out a song of *Bravura*, the subject of which was the castration of the devil by a baker; (which, by the bye, is a very curious story, whose authenticity I must enquire into farther at my leisure.) I immediately augured my approaching destiny from the burden of this song; and the *Cornuto* presently gave me to understand that my conjecture was well founded. Having been till now in a cold-sweat, and corporal fear of my life, I congratulated myself on this exchange of punishment, as a sort of reprieve, and considering that I had some

time

time ſince reſolved, like another *Graſſetto*, to undergo the operation whenever I found myſelf bold enough for ſuch a voluntary ſacrifice ; I plucked up courage, and with great compoſure told the barber, that a guilty conſcience was a greater torment to me than any he could deviſe ; but that to expiate the crime I had committed, and appeaſe the anger of heaven, and the honeſt man whom I had ſo deeply offended, I would patiently ſubmit to ſuffer the righteous ſentence which his vengeance meditated on the peccant part. The enraged tonſor took me at my word.

* * * * * * * * *

The firſt thing that came into my thoughts after I awoke from the fainting fit, into which the paroxiſm of pain had thrown me, was to try my voice in its improved ſtate. I accordingly ſung *A Dawn of Hope my Soul revives*, and found my powers wonderfully improved, and my execution delicate, intereſting, and full of effects. " Ho, ho," cries the barber, " I

" am glad to find you are ſo merry," and reſumed his old tune of the baker and the devil. I told him I thought it unkind in him to inſult me, and intreated him to convey me home, which he very readily conſented to do, and ſoon afterwards began to apolcgize for the effects of his rage, hoping I would conſider the nature of the provocation, and not attempt to take the law of him. I anſwered, that upon condition he would freely pardon his wife, whoſe fault was venial, as her virtue had fallen a ſacrifice to the power of harmony, I would decline any hoſtile proceedings againſt him on my own account, with which condition he appeared ſatisfied, and we parted.—I was brought home on a mule, on which I rode ſideways; and as ſoon as I alighted at Signor *Manſelli*'s I ſent for him into my chamber, and accoſted him as a he approached with the following air, in ſinging which I exerted all my newly-acquired powers.

*Bear*

*Bear, O bear me on a ſudden,*
*Some kind ſtroke of ſmiling chance!*
*From this land of beef and pudding,*
*To dear* Italy *or* France!

*I am ſick to the ſoul,*
*Politics and ſea-coal,*
*So give one the vapours,*
*Their curſed news-papers,*
*Their mobbing,*
*Stock-jobbing*
*Are horrors to me;*
*I wiſh the whole iſland were ſunk in*
*the ſea.*

During my performance, the Signor appeared perfectly aſtoniſhed, and at length ſeizing my hand with rapture, " welcome," he cried, " O ſon of harmony! it cannot " be longer diſguiſed, you are a brother— " you are one of us"—then expatiating on the dignity and importance of the order of *caſtrati,* he deſired me, if not too much exhauſted, to ſing again his favourite air, which when I had done he he cried out with transport;—"*nec vox* "*hominem sonat!* I can hardly believe "it is the same pipe! such a volume of "voice, such an open and perfect shake! "such light and shade! never was voice "less *cloudy!* such clearness, brilliancy, "neatness, expression, embellishment, in- "tonation, firmness, modulation, smooth- "ness and elegance! and then your *por-* "*tamento* is as round and tight as a "portmanteau, and you take *appogiatura*, "as easily as a body would take a pinch "of snuff!"—

I was greatly flattered by these encomiums, but begged he would forbear and suffer me to retire to my chamber, for the sake of necessary refreshment and rest. He immediately complied, and sent up to me Signor *Sougelder*, an eminent surgeon in the neighbourhood, and an agreeable performer on the *English* horn; who having applied an excellent dressing to my wound left me to sleep, and "thus "ended this busy and important day, in

"which

"which ſo much was ſaid, and done, "that it ſeemed to contain the events of a "much longer period; and I could hardly "perſuade myſelf, upon recollecting the "ſeveral incidents, that they had all hap-"pened in about the ſpace of twelve "hours." By the kind and ſkilful offices of Signor *Sougelder*, I was ſoon reſtored to my health and ſpirits; and my adorable Signora *Gluckinelli* in a few days paid me a viſit of congratulation, which ſhe repeated every day during my recovery. It was in ſome of theſe delightful interviews I diſcovered how deep a theoriſt ſhe was, and how learned in the ſcience of ſound. Among other diſcoveries and obſervations which ſhe communicated to me, and which I treaſure up, and mean to preſerve for the benefit of future ages, ſhe aſſured me that it was "practicable "with time and patience to give a ſhake "where nature has denied it; that ſhe "thought, the ſhake ruined ninety-nine "times out of a hundred by too much "impatience and precipitation, both in "the master and scholar, and that many "who can execute passages which require "the same motion of the *larynx* as the shake, "have notwithstanding never acquired "one"—"There is no accounting for "this," added that illustrious young lady, with a sigh, "but from the neglect of "the master to study nature, and avail "himself of these passages, which by "continuity would become real shakes."

During my confinement to my chamber, I have had leisure to extract the foregoing observations, anecdotes, and adventures, from my journal, and which I present to the world as the first hints of my undertaking. If they tend in any shape to promote the study and practice of music in this country, and by that means lessen our national reproach of being *The savages of Europe*, immersed in politics, philosophy, metaphysics, mathematics, and other sour and abstruse speculations, I shall have gained my

end,

end, and shall congratulate myself on having in some humble degree assisted the generous efforts of the great musical Doctor, and the governors of the *Foundling Hospital*, to polish and *Italianize* the genius, taste, and manners of the *English* nation.

I shall trespass on the reader's patience but one moment longer, to inform him that as soon as I had perfectly recovered my health, Signor *Manselli* instituted a grand *Fête Champêtre* to celebrate what he was pleased to call my victory over the flesh and the devil; and to crown the whole, the idol of my soul, the fair *Gluckinella*, was that day pleased to condescend publicly to avow her platonic harmonic passion for me; and to promise me in the most endearing manner, that if ever she entered into the holy state of matrimony, I should be her CECISBEO.

THE END.

*Speedily will be published;*

# An ENQUIRY into the PRESENT STATE

OF THE

# MUSIC OF THE SPHERES.

To which will be prefixed,

The OVERTURE to the last ECLIPSE of the MOON;

And, a Dissertation on the Structure and Use

OF THE

CELESTIAL BOW, commonly called the RAIN-BOW.

---

By JOEL COLLIER, Organist.

---

*Avia Pieridum perago loca nullius antè*
*Trita solo.* LUCR.

---

*** Price to Subscribers, Two Guineas; Non-Subscribers Three Guineas and an Half.

* 9 7 8 0 2 5 9 8 0 7 0 0 1 *

SD - #0149 - 150424 - C0 - 229/152/4 - PB - 9780259807001 - Gloss Lamination